The Bloody Wake
of the *Infamy*

by
Anne Schraff

Perfection Learning® Corporation
Logan, Iowa 51546

Editor: Pegi Bevins
Cover Illustration: Doug Knutson
Cover Design: Deborah Lea Bell
Michael A. Aspengren

For information, contact
Perfection Learning® Corporation
1000 North Second Avenue, P.O. Box 500
Logan, Iowa 51546-0500.
Tel: 1-800-831-4190 • Fax: 1-712-644-2392
Paperback ISBN 0-7891-5240-1
Cover Craft® ISBN 0-7807-9650-0
Printed in the U.S.A.

1 Peter McCall was 16 in 1760 when he boarded his father's merchant ship for the voyage to England. Peter had been aboard his father's ship before. He had climbed the boarding nets and walked the decks since he was a toddler. But never before had he joined his father for a voyage across the Atlantic Ocean. And he was looking forward to the adventure. When Peter reached England, he would be going to school in Cambridge.

"You will return to Boston a well-educated man," his father had promised. "The schools in England are far superior to those in the colonies."

Peter's father, Edmund McCall, was a sea merchant. He had made a considerable fortune carrying goods to European ports from around the world. The family lived on a large estate near Boston, Massachusetts, in a stately mansion surrounded by green fields and fragrant pine woods.

Earlier that morning, Mrs. McCall had blinked back her tears and bade a sad farewell to her only son. "I will miss you,

Peter," she said, planting a gentle kiss on the boy's forehead.

"I'll miss you too, Mother," Peter replied, struggling to hold back his own tears.

"But I know it's all for your good, so I must be brave," his mother smiled. "Will you promise to write to us?"

"I promise," Peter said. "I will write every week. You'll see."

His mother had embraced him quickly then and turned away. He was sure that she didn't want him to see her crying. Peter had turned away too. He didn't want his mother to know that he, too, had lost the battle against his tears.

But now the sad farewell was behind him, and Peter couldn't help being excited about the upcoming journey. He would miss his mother, he knew, but he would keep his promise and stay in touch through letters.

Later that morning, the *Camille*, Mr. McCall's ship, left Boston harbor with her sails filled with a brisk wind. Edmund McCall shouted, "We are off to an auspicious start already, my boy!"

But the beginning of the journey was not as good for Peter. As he strolled around the deck, enjoying the feel of the ship gliding through the water, he felt unfriendly eyes upon him. Looking up, he saw one of the crew members glaring at him from the ropes above. The sailor was in his twenties, with muscular arms and skin that was bronzed from the sun. Tattoos of various designs covered both arms—forked-tongued dragons, spiders, and human skulls. In his teeth the man held a knife. Peter could see the sharp blade flashing in the sunlight.

"Hello," Peter called, hoping to appear friendly. He had never seen this sailor before. He figured the man was probably one of the new sailors his father had signed on for the journey.

The man did not bother to answer Peter. He continued to glare at the boy as he adjusted one of the riggings. As he did so, the knife in his teeth dropped to the deck below. Its sharp blade stuck into the boards at Peter's feet.

Peter gasped. The knife had barely missed him! He glanced back up at the man, whose eyes were now full of cruel amusement. It was obvious he found the incident humorous. But had he meant to hit him? Peter wondered.

Suddenly the man leaped down from the ropes, as quick as a hawk pouncing on its prey. He landed on all fours directly in front of Peter. The man grabbed the knife and stood up. Then he said with a sneer, "So you're Peter McCall, eh?"

As he spoke, he held the knife out at a threatening angle.

"Y-yes," Peter stammered. "Who . . . who are you?"

"My name is Oliver," the man replied. "Riley Oliver. I don't suppose you recognize the name." He spoke this as if it was an accusation.

Peter searched his mind. He was sure he didn't know this man. "No, sh-should I?" he asked. He stared down at the knife, which was now only a few inches from his midsection.

Oliver spat derisively on the deck. "Like as not," he growled, moving the knife slightly closer.

The man terrified Peter. Who was he?

Peter wondered. And what had Peter done to deserve his hatred?

Peter was at a loss to answer either question. But he knew he had to get away from this Riley Oliver, whoever he was. Peter thought quickly. "I . . . I'd better be going now, Mr. Oliver," he said. "I promised my father I would dine with him."

Riley Oliver's scowl grew deeper. He moved his face close to Peter's, seemingly boring his hatred into the boy with his eyes. "Dine with him, eh?" he said. "I don't expect you'll be eating the fare the rest of us will, *Peter McCall*!" He spit out Peter's name as if he were trying to rid his mouth of a rotten piece of meat. "Since your father is the captain, you can dine on delicacies at the captain's table. While the rest of us chew on biscuits full of weevils, and salt pork hard enough to break a man's skull if you hit him with it."

It was true. The McCalls had a well-stocked cabin to make their journey more comfortable. But surely Father does not expect the crew to eat such food as this man describes! Peter thought. This man must be lying.

"Aye, but don't worry your head, lad," Oliver went on. "We have rancid grog to wash down the slop."

He stepped away from Peter then, allowing the boy to pass. Unnerved by the man's bitterness, Peter left the deck. He went to the captain's cabin where he found his father making entries into the ship's log.

"Father, I was just talking to one of the crew. He was complaining fiercely about the food. He spoke of wormy biscuits and stony salt pork," Peter said.

Mr. McCall laughed and said, "Indeed, if those lazy louts had nothing to complain about, they wouldn't be happy!"

Peter said nothing. Maybe so, he thought. Maybe the sailor was making it all up. But the man certainly hadn't been making up the hatred he felt toward Peter. Riley Oliver's hatred had been as true as the love Peter felt for his own family. But Peter said nothing to Mr. McCall of his encounter with Oliver. He didn't want his father to think him a complainer so early in the voyage.

"Have you worked up a hunger yet,

Peter?" Mr. McCall asked. "We have fresh meat. It will not be for several days that we shall have to eat salted provisions."

Peter felt a little guilty at the thought of enjoying the savory beef. If what Oliver had said was true, the rest of the crew was eating food fit for dogs. "No, I guess I'm not hungry," he replied.

Mr. McCall saw the concern lingering on his son's face and laughed again. "Do not be so gullible, Peter. Men such as we hire to work aboard the *Camille* are the dregs of society. They know nothing but to complain because they are by their natures lazy and good-for-nothing. Do not listen to them. What they say is of less meaning than the shrieks of the gulls."

Now Peter smiled too. His father was probably right. Sailors were recruited from the ranks of the poor and uneducated. They carried their worldly goods in a kerchief and rarely took baths or shaved, as a gentleman would. In the past, Peter had often seen them sleeping in hammocks slung between the decks of the *Camille*—right out in the open air! Men of such slovenly behavior were probably not to be believed, Peter thought as he joined his father at the table.

* * *

The *Camille* made good time that day. The winds were good, billowing out the sails like clouds as the ship sped along. The feel of the wind on his face made Peter almost forget the unpleasant encounter he'd had with Riley Oliver.

Midafternoon Peter and his father were on deck talking about Peter's schooling at Cambridge University.

"Cambridge is a fine school, Peter," Mr. McCall said. "Men of the McCall family have been educated there for the past 200 years."

"I'm looking forward to it, Father," Peter said. At the university, he was to study medicine. Peter planned to be a doctor someday. His grandfather had gotten him interested in herbal medicine long ago. The older man often took Peter walking in the fields and meadows of Massachusetts, looking for certain plants. Abraham McCall had the ability to cure most ills with a tonic, powder, or poultice made from herbs. And he had passed this knowledge on to Peter. As a result, herbal medicine had become a serious hobby for Peter. He had even filled his sea chest with books of herbal remedies to study on the voyage to England.

"Yes, you will be well-educated in medicine when you return to Massachusetts," Mr. McCall said. "Cambridge is one of the finest science universities in the world. You are leaving here a mere boy, Peter, and will return to us a fine doctor."

Peter smiled and hoped his father was right.

Suddenly they heard a shout from the crow's nest far above. "Ship ahoy! Ship ahoy!" the sailor called.

Peter shielded his eyes from the bright sun and looked in the direction the sailor was pointing. A great schooner was coming from behind, sending out huge waves before it. Peter could read the words *Infamy* on the side of the ship. On the flag flying high above the vessel, he made out the image of a skull and crossbones—the symbol of pirates! As Peter watched in terror and fascination, he saw that the guns of the *Infamy* were pointed right at the *Camille*.

"We are under attack!" Edmund McCall cried in astonishment. "To your guns, men!"

Suddenly Peter could hear the roar of cannon balls above him. The crew of the *Camille* hastened to the big guns and began shooting back. Cannons from both ships spouted fire, but the larger pirate vessel had the advantage, having many more guns. Soon the *Infamy* shredded the spars and rigging of the *Camille*. Within minutes, it was clear that the pirate ship had overwhelmed the smaller one.

The schooner now pulled alongside the *Camille*. Out of the smoke and fire of the attack, pirates clambered onto the wounded ship. They scrambled up the boarding nets, waving their cutlasses and pistols.

As Peter stared in disbelief, fighting broke out all around him. The crew of the *Camille* fought valiantly for the ship but was both outnumbered and outskilled. In horror, Peter watched as one of the pirates sliced at a crew member, deftly parting the man's head from his body.

"Get below, Peter!" Mr. McCall shouted, but it was too late. Just as the boy started to head for the cabin below deck, a pirate leaped up behind him and began dragging him backward. Peter felt the cold steel of a knife blade against his throat.

"Unhand the boy!" Mr. McCall shouted, running up. Suddenly he stopped and stood staring at the man holding Peter.

"Edmund McCall, you old devil!" cried the pirate. "I've got your son, and I'll kill him with pleasure!"

Even though Peter couldn't see the man, he recognized the voice. It was Riley Oliver! He had joined the attacking pirates. So this was why he had signed on in Boston. He had probably told the pirates exactly where to find the *Camille*.

"Unhand my son!" Mr. McCall repeated to the traitor.

"Nay," Oliver cried, "I shall behead him first, sir, and lash his handsome head to our bowsprit!"

Captain Edmund McCall's face went

white with terror. He shouted for his crew to cease all resistance and to give the pirates what they asked for. The men stopped fighting. Instantly every member of the crew had a pirate with a pistol or cutlass in hand standing over him.

"Take whatever you want, Oliver," Peter's father pleaded. "Just let the boy go."

Just then a tall man with a hawk nose and an ugly scar on his face stepped forward. "I am Robert Foster, captain of the *Infamy*," he said. "We are not here to take your cargo, sir. Sugar and cotton are not worth my time." He glanced at Oliver, still holding the knife to Peter's throat. "Oliver here tells me you're a wealthy man."

"That's right," Riley Oliver said. "He's one of the richest men in Massachusetts. His family lives in a grand manner—like royalty. I have seen the carriages taking them to and from their amusements, with the family coat of arms on the sides of the chaises."

Captain Foster looked at Peter's father again. "How much gold will you pay for your son's life?" he asked.

Edmund McCall looked in panic from Peter to Captain Foster as he realized what was going on. "I . . . I will get whatever you ask," he stammered. "On my sacred honor, I swear I will get the money from my bankers. But first you must free my son."

The wild laughter of the pirates at this demand mingled with the sound of the roaring sea. Peter was dizzy with terror. He feared that standing on the rolling deck with the knife at his throat would result in his accidental, if not intended, murder.

Captain Foster nodded to two nearby pirates, who then surrounded Peter. They pulled his arms behind him and bound his wrists with ropes. Then they shoved him toward the edge of the deck at the point of a cutlass.

"You cannot take my son," Mr. McCall shouted. But even as his father spoke, Peter was dragged over the side and onto the deck of the *Infamy*.

Peter knew his father could do nothing to help him. If Mr. McCall sent his crew into action to resume the fighting, many men would die.

As Captain Foster left the smaller ship, he shouted to Peter's father, "I will contact you about the ransom. Await my message!"

In the dusk, Peter looked sadly across the water at the *Camille*. The ship sat motionless, its sails torn, its rigging in a tangle. It would require much work to get the vessel seaworthy again. When it finally limped back into Boston harbor, Peter knew his father would do everything in his power to meet the ransom demand. But would he get the money quickly enough to satisfy the violent robbers? Peter wondered. Or would they kill him anyway?

2 "Look, the laddie wears a handsome coat!" one of the pirates who had bound Peter's wrists sneered. He gave Peter a shove that sent him to his knees on the deck.

"Seth Hanes, you are a fool!" snarled another pirate. "You'll tear the coat knocking it about like that. The size looks just right for me!"

"Don't just stand there, Josh Manley! Help me untie the boy, and we'll see who gets the coat!" Seth ordered.

Captain Foster and Riley Oliver stood by in amusement as the two men untied Peter and roughly yanked off his coat. Then they began quarreling over it.

"You have the arms of an ape," Josh snarled. "The sleeves are too short for you!"

But Seth insisted on trying on Peter's coat. When he saw that his arms stuck awkwardly out of the sleeves, he ripped the coat in rage. For a few seconds, Josh and Seth wrestled on the deck of the ship. Finally Captain Foster threatened them both with his pistol.

"You know the regulations," he said.

"No man may strike another aboard the ship. If you have a quarrel, wait until we go ashore and then settle it."

As Peter watched what was happening, he was sickened to the depths of his soul. He had never been so close to such violent, raw men before. They reminded him of wild beasts battling over an animal carcass.

Peter continued to stare longingly at the *Camille* as he sailed away on the *Infamy*. He thought he could see his father standing on deck watching him, but he couldn't be sure. Soon the merchant ship was gone from sight as the distance and the darkness swallowed it up. Now Peter's despair was complete. There was nothing now but the grinning, sneering, and often deformed faces of the captors around him.

Josh Manley was a gaunt man with one blue eye and the other covered by a black patch. He wore a gold earring in one ear and a heavy chain of gold around his neck. Seth Hanes was stout with a great, humped nose that looked as if it had been broken several times. His eyes were as bloodshot red as the bandanna he wore around his head. A heavyset man called Eli Cooper had broken brown teeth and stringy black hair. His stubbly beard was streaked with gray, and his thick eyebrows met in a dark ridge above his nose. The man they called Liam West was a giant of a man, with arms as thick as hams. His back and chest rippled with muscles, and the calves of his legs strained against the high boots he wore, as if they would snap the laces. Like Riley Oliver, hideous tattoos covered the pirates' arms and backs. Liam West even had the image of an evil-looking serpent coiled around his neck and slithering up onto his face.

"Laddie," Seth urged with a mischievous grin, "tell us about your grand life in Boston. Tell us about the dainties you enjoy at the table."

Peter opened his mouth to speak. But he found that his mouth was so dry from fear that he could barely manage a whisper. He shook his head and croaked, "I cannot speak."

Immediately Riley Oliver whipped out his knife. "If I were to cut out your tongue, *then* you could not speak," he hissed. "But until I do so, you will! Now answer the man's question. Tell us about the fine foods you enjoyed at your table."

"Yes, tell us, did you dine on turtle soup? On green turtle soup in fine china bowls?" Seth asked mockingly. He then took out his own pistol and pointed it at Peter. "Speak now, boy. Nothing would give me more pleasure than to put a hole through that pretty head of yours!"

"Enough, you louts! Back to work!" Captain Foster roared. "No one is to touch the boy. We must keep him alive until we collect the ransom from his father. McCall might demand proof that his son still lives." He looked at Peter and laughed then. "Once we have our gold—*then* you may do with him as you like!"

Peter's heart sank. So they're going to kill me after all, he thought in despair. My father will give them everything he's worked so hard for—and still they will murder his only son. My poor father. If only there were a way I could tell him. But it was useless, Peter knew. He had no way to send word to his father. Then he remembered the promise he had made his mother—to write home once a week. Not only would he not be writing home, he thought. But more than likely, he would never even see her or his father again.

As the crew got back to the business of running the ship, Peter was, for the most part, ignored. A boy of a mere 16 years was no threat to them, even with his hands free. The only person who paid any attention to him was Riley Oliver. Oliver worked nearby, frequently looking distrustfully at Peter. Peter sank to the deck and leaned back against a barrel to await the inevitable—his eventual death.

For the next hour or so, the schooner hugged the coast in the darkness. Finally it put in at a place called Gardiners Island. The island lay in Long Island Sound and was owned by an Englishman who tolerated pirates.

As soon as the ship dropped anchor, Captain Foster ordered that Peter be taken to a cabin below deck and locked in. Riley Oliver led the boy into the darkness of the lower level and shoved him into one of the compartments.

"Sweet dreams, *Mr.* McCall!" he sneered,

slamming the door. Peter heard the click of the lock as Oliver turned the key.

Turning around, Peter found himself in a small room, no more than six feet long and four feet wide. The ceiling was so low that he had to stoop to avoid hitting his head. At one end of the cabin was a sort of shelf with a dirty blanket and pillow on it. Peter assumed it was the bed. The idea of sleeping on such a makeshift cot repulsed him. He was used to plush feather beds and fluffy goose down pillows. But as he stood in the dimness of the room, he realized how exhausted he was. The events of the day had taken their toll on him, and he wanted desperately to sleep.

With a resigned sigh, he took off his boots and pulled back the blanket on the bed. Then he lay down and covered himself. He almost choked from the musty smell of the pillow and thought he would never fall asleep with such an odor in his nose. But his weariness and the gentle rocking of the ship soon overcame his aversion. He drifted off, thinking about Riley Oliver and wondering why the pirate hated him so much.

He had only been asleep a few minutes when he felt something move against his leg. Instantly he was wide awake, his heart beating wildly as he threw the blanket back. In the dim light, he could see something dark scurry off his bed. He had been sharing his bed with a rat! He reached down, picked up his boot, and hurled it wildly in the direction the rat had gone. Then all was quiet. The unwanted visitor had evidently escaped into a hole in the wall.

He lay back down on the bed, shaken by the experience. He had never confronted a rat before, much less had one in his bed. The smell of the pillow made him cough again, and he slapped at his arm after feeling a sharp bite on his skin. A flea, no doubt, he thought. He knew that where there were rats, there were most certainly fleas. He wondered how he would ever adjust to such loathsome conditions even if the pirates let him live.

It took him much longer the second time, but finally Peter McCall slept again. He awakened to the sound of bells. Bells, he knew, indicated the change of watch on a ship. Some of the crew would retire to their beds, and others would take over their duties.

A few minutes later, he heard the key turn in the lock. Riley Oliver opened the door and growled, "Captain Foster says you're to come to breakfast."

Peter put on his boots and followed the man up to the mess where the crew ate. Each man was given a plate of salted meat and hardtack biscuits. It was crude fare, but at least Peter saw no worms in the biscuits. He was hungry and managed to eat a little. He washed it down with weak, bitter coffee from a bent tin cup.

The pirates around him ate ravenously. They used their fingers almost like shovels and filled their mouths until food spilled over their lips. Peter stared at the men in dismay. Again he was reminded of wild animals. But a few minutes later, Peter noticed that Eli Cooper was clutching his ample stomach. "My belly!" he moaned. "My belly is killing me with pain!"

As Eli moaned, an idea came to Peter.

His grandfather had taught him how to ease indigestion using a plant called wormwood. Perhaps if he could go ashore, he could find some wormwood and help Eli Cooper. And, Peter thought, if he was allowed to wander the fields in search of the plant, he just might have a chance to escape.

"I have knowledge of herbs that can ease the man's stomachache," Peter told Riley Oliver, who was sitting nearby.

Oliver sneered and said, "It's just a trick to get ashore and escape. What would a boy like you know of medicine?"

"My grandfather taught me much in the way of healing herbs," Peter explained. "On my father's ship, I had an entire chest full of books and remedies."

"Bah!" Oliver barked.

But Eli Cooper, upon hearing Peter, stumbled over to the boy. "Could you honestly prepare a medicine for my pain?" he asked.

"I might be able to," the boy offered nervously.

"I'll ask the captain for permission to take you ashore," Eli said.

A few minutes later, he was back with Captain Foster.

"What's this I hear about you being a healer, boy?" the captain asked Peter.

"My grandfather taught me herbal remedies," Peter said.

Foster looked doubtful but said to Seth Hanes and Josh Manley, "All right, take young McCall ashore. Let him search for these herbs of his. If he tries to escape, catch him and remove his ears from his head! For if he gets away, you shall both pay. I will cut out your hearts with my cutlass!"

Peter shuddered at the captain's words. He did not doubt that these brutal men would slash off his ears if he tried to get away. He resolved to attempt to escape only if he was fairly certain that he would not be caught.

A rowboat was lowered, and the three climbed in and went ashore. The two pirates stayed close behind Peter as he roamed the fields. It took him about 15 minutes to spot the plant he was after.

"There," he said at last. "There's the wormwood I need."

"Get it then and be quick about it," Josh growled. "But if it does not ease the fat man's pain, he may tear out a handful of your hair."

As Peter pulled a few of the plants out of the ground, he thought back to the days with his grandfather. He remembered going into the woods and collecting various plants—strawberry and basil, wild rose, garlic and hops, cowslip flowers and roots. One summer, one of the McCalls' servants was severely injured when a wagon wheel that he was fixing fell on his leg. Grandfather had healed the wound with a poultice of agrimony and the pulp of a bryony root.

Peter's grandfather had died last year. Now Peter wondered what Abraham McCall would think of his grandson using the knowledge he had gained from the old man to help a pirate.

"Hurry up!" Josh barked. "Another minute and I'll take one of your ears— even if you don't try to escape!"

Peter looked around. The two pirates were only a few feet away. It would be futile, he knew, to run. He picked what he needed then and returned with the two men to the ship.

On board again, Peter put the blossoms and leaves of the wormwood into a pot of water. Slowly he boiled the mixture over a small fire until he had a strong tonic. After cooling the tonic, he poured the brown liquid into a tin cup.

"Here, this should ease your pain," he said, handing the cup to Eli Cooper.

Cooper gulped the tonic and sank to the floor to rest. Some of the other men watched with interest. Riley Oliver continued to sneer, doubtful that the tonic would benefit Eli.

"Has the pain eased, Eli?" Seth asked. "Have you been made well?"

Eli was silent for a moment. Then he said in a slow, thoughtful voice, "The pain is not gone, but it *is* better, methinks. I do believe it did me good."

Peter felt a small measure of relief. At least he had demonstrated a useful skill to these vicious men. Perhaps now they would see some benefit in keeping him alive.

Eli improved still more. As he regarded

Peter through watery, bloodshot eyes, he asked, "How did you come by such wondrous knowledge?"

"My grandfather healed with herbs," Peter explained. "He was very fond of me, and I was his constant companion as a young boy. From him I learned how to find useful herbs and how to prepare them."

"You're a kind of physician then?" Eli asked.

Peter hesitated. He didn't want to claim to be more than he was. If they tested him and found him wanting, he would probably be hung from the yardarm high above the deck. Yet Peter wanted to make himself as valuable as possible to help preserve his life.

"I'm not a physician," he began cautiously, "but where there is no doctor, I can help ease many kinds of maladies."

"My stomach has plagued me for many years," Eli said. "The tonic you made offered me the first relief I've had."

"Your bellyache cured itself, Cooper," Riley Oliver declared. "This braggart had nothing to do with it. He's a deceiver."

Eli glared at Oliver and replied, "It was *my* belly that was hurting, not yours. And I know what I feel. We could use someone on board with such skills as the lad has."

"If you did not eat like a pig, you would not suffer such stomach pains," Oliver said.

Eli fingered the hilt of his cutlass menacingly. "I have endured enough of your insults, Oliver!" he threatened

But the younger pirate just laughed and walked away, saying, "You're not worth fighting, Eli."

Later in the day, two sailors brought back fish they had caught in nets off Gardiners Island. The fish were roasted, and the fragrant smell drifted across the decks of the schooner.

Eli Cooper brought some of the fish to Peter and said, "Eat hearty, lad. We may have need of your services after we do battle with the next ship we find."

The fish was surprisingly delicious, and Peter ate it quickly. He realized that in Eli Cooper he now had a sort of ally. Someone who thought him valuable enough to keep alive because of his skills.

But a little later that evening, the pirates began drinking rum in great quantities. This raised fresh fears in Peter's heart. How much good would his new friendship do him if the pirates, including Eli, became blind drunk? What if one of them—like Riley Oliver—set upon him? Would any of the others help him?

Then, slowly, hope rose in Peter's heart. Would the pirates get so drunk that he could escape? he wondered. Many of them were already unsteady on their feet. Could he slip away without their noticing? And, if so, where would he go? There was no point in heading out on his own because he had no idea where the next island lay. So he had no choice but to go back to Gardiners Island. He wondered how big the island was. Perhaps it was not even big enough to hide him. But Peter decided it was worth taking a chance. Anything was better than remaining with such hooligans.

Peter watched the drunken men dance about in wild jigs as one of them began to play a fiddle. Nobody was guarding him now. No one even seemed aware that he was there.

When the moon crept behind a bank of clouds, Peter got to his feet. Cautiously and as quietly as possible, he lowered a rowboat into the water. He glanced behind him at the revelry. So far, so good. Some of the men were singing loudly now, covering up any noise he made.

Peter climbed down the boarding net of the ship and dropped into the small boat. He rowed toward the island, his oars silently slicing the still water. A few minutes later, he reached the shoreline. The water sloshed softly on the sand as he tied the boat to a sapling. In the distance Peter saw a stand of trees and some broken-down fences and animal sheds. He headed that way.

Suddenly he heard a shout from the *Infamy*. "Where's the boy?" Peter didn't recognize the voice, but it carried easily through the still night.

"One of the rowboats is gone!" another yelled.

"After him!" This time Peter knew who had spoken. It was Riley Oliver.

3 By the light of the moon, Peter could see several men clambering down the boarding net of the schooner. Peter broke into a run, heading for the stand of trees that would provide him with cover.

Peter was awash in perspiration as he crouched in the trees. He knew that Captain Foster would send out the entire crew, if necessary, to find him. Peter was worth a lot of money to Foster, and the pirate was not about to give that up. He recalled Captain Foster's words, *If he tries to escape, catch him and remove his ears from his head!*

Fear of being recaptured made Peter almost nauseous. His mind worked feverishly for a way to escape.

"Spread out!" he heard Riley Oliver command. "The island is not more than a mile square. We'll find him sooner or later."

As Peter had feared, the island was too small to conceal him for long. Even if he was able to hide for the night, they'd surely find him the next day. He decided he had no choice but to go back to the ship with the pirates. He would attempt another escape when the opportunity presented itself. In the meantime, he had to think of a way to keep from getting his ears cut off when the pirates caught up with him.

Peter looked behind him at the same field where he had found the wormwood. He stood up in the moonlight and began slowly walking into the field, making a kind of sack from the handkerchief he had in his pocket. He spotted some verbena plants and picked them, depositing them into his makeshift sack.

"There he is!" a man yelled.

Peter turned and saw Captain Foster himself approaching, cutlass in hand. Peter swallowed back his terror. He said in as calm a voice as he could muster, "I need an herb sack. Eli Cooper told me I should be prepared in case any of the men are injured in the next raid. I've gathered some verbena already, but there are other beneficial plants here that I need."

Captain Foster let loose with a roar of laughter. "He's gathering medicinal herbs!" he shouted. "The fool is building an herb sack by the light of the moon!"

The other men ran up to join their

captain. Some muttered in disbelief at the boy's foolishness, and others shook their heads. But all seemed to accept Peter's explanation—all except Riley Oliver. He glared knowingly at Peter, indicating with his eyes that he suspected the real reason the boy had gone to the island.

"Stay with the boy, Oliver," Captain Foster commanded. "See that he gets his herbs. Then bring him back to the ship. We sail at dawn!"

Once the others had gone, Riley Oliver said, "You fooled the rest of them, but you didn't fool me. You were trying to escape. And just so it doesn't happen again, I'll use my strongest knots to lash your ankles together from now on!"

Peter stared at the other man who was only about four or five years older than he. His hatred for Peter seemed to be an ever-burning furnace within him.

"Tell me," Peter said, "since we only met, what have I done to deserve your hatred? I don't even know you, and you surely do not know me."

" 'Tis true that I hate you, McCall," Oliver said bluntly. "You are the son of

Edmund McCall, and that is reason enough for my hatred. I should like nothing better than to send a rowboat into Boston Bay carrying your bones picked clean by vultures. Ah, for the sight of your father's face when he beheld what was left of his only son! I would gladly forfeit 10 years of my life!"

"Do you hate my father because he is wealthy?" Peter asked.

Riley Oliver's voice became the low growl of an animal. "Do you know of debtors' prison?" he asked.

"I have heard of it," Peter said.

"My father died in a stone cold debtors' prison," Oliver seethed. "He died in filthy conditions, with no one to even hold up his head while he died."

"Why was he in debtors' prison?" Peter asked.

"My father was a tinsmith who was befallen by bad times," the pirate replied. "He always paid his debts, but there came a time when he could not. He had a wife and four children, and he did the best he could."

"What does that have to do with my father?" Peter asked.

"My father owed a small sum to Edmund McCall, and he wrote your father a letter, pleading that he not press demands for repayment," Oliver said. "My father offered to pay the principal on the amount if only he could wait on the interest. But it was not to be."

"Surely my father did not press the demand for repayment if he knew the circumstances," Peter said.

Angrily, the pirate replied, "Your father refused to be merciful! Phineas Oliver was sent to debtors' prison until he paid McCall what he owed—which he could not do. How could he pay when he was in prison? In the meantime, my sisters and I starved while my mother tried desperately to find food. We were cold and hungry and lived on other people's garbage."

Oliver closed his eyes then, as if the memory was too painful to face. Then he went on. "Eventually, two of my sisters perished, and our mother died coughing up blood. I was left alone at 14 with my 10-year-old sister. We were the only survivors of your father's cruelty. And that is why I hate Edmund McCall and will to my dying day. That is why I have sworn vengeance against him. And the best way to do it is to take from him his dearest possession, his youngest child and only son!"

That's not possible, Peter thought to himself. His father was a hard businessman, it was true. But he would never demand the imprisonment of a debtor who pleaded for mercy. He would never doom a poor family to hunger and disease.

The young pirate was a liar! He had the story all wrong. What could Peter expect from a scoundrel like Riley Oliver anyway? He was surely attempting to excuse his own wicked life by pinning the blame on decent men.

But Peter said nothing. He knew that Oliver was capable—even desirous—of killing him. He didn't want to anger him any further. So Peter kept his silence and hoped that someday all of the pirates from the *Infamy* would be brought to justice before the Admiralty Court.

He finished gathering a few more plants and then returned to the ship with Oliver.

In the morning, the *Infamy* sailed south and put in at a deserted beach on the coast of South Carolina. A decaying old mansion stood in the distance, surrounded by a corral of horses. Peter supposed that the pirates paid a fee to lie low here.

As the ship neared the beach, Peter saw where there had been bonfires on the sand. This was obviously a pirates' lair. A place where many businessmen came to make deals on the booty stolen by pirates. Such men did not care how the goods were obtained, as long as there was a profit to be made.

The crew dropped anchor and lowered the rowboats into the water. Then all the men, including Peter, went ashore.

"I'll take one of the horses from Thatcher's corral here and ride to Boston," Captain Foster said as they climbed out of the small boats. "I'll make sure that Edmund McCall knows he must pay a king's ransom, or he will one day find his bonny boy a corpse!"

This brought raucous laughter from some of the pirates. Seth Hanes said,

"Captain, who's in charge while you're gone? Name one of us to lead this motley crew!"

Captain Foster's gaze swept over the men, resting for a few seconds on Josh Manley and finally settling on Riley Oliver. "Oliver, are you man enough to handle this bunch of barbarians?" he asked.

"Aye, that I am," Oliver replied confidently.

"Is any man opposed to Riley Oliver taking the wheel while I'm gone?" Foster asked the group.

There was some general grumbling among some of the men, but no real objections were raised.

The captain nodded and said, "So be it. Oliver, you're in charge while I'm gone. Make sure there's no fighting on the ship and that the booty is shared equally."

"That I'll do, Captain," Oliver assured him.

Peter looked at Josh Manley. He was scowling at Riley Oliver, his one eye squinted in hatred. Peter watched as Manley kicked a pile of sand and stalked off.

"I'll be back in a carriage loaded with gold," Captain Foster called over his shoulder as he headed for the corral. "Or I'll be back astride my horse, and you will know the rich man refused to pay. Then we will decide what end to make of Peter McCall!"

A few minutes later, Peter watched him gallop off on a bay horse, headed north.

Eli Cooper turned to Peter and said, "Have you ever been fishing, boy?"

"Yes, I used to fish with my grandfather," Peter replied.

"Come along then," Eli said. "I'm tired of salt pork and hard biscuits. Let's catch some fish and fry them on the beach."

"Make sure he does not escape," Riley Oliver warned as the two headed off. "If he escapes through your stupidity, I swear I will take it out of your hide, Eli Cooper!"

"Ahhh," Eli snarled at Oliver, "I've been a buccaneer since before you were born, laddie. I've lost neither booty nor prisoner in all that time."

He grinned at Peter then and headed for the rowboats. He was an ugly, sloppy man, with more teeth missing than remained in his head. Strands of long, dirty hair lay across his brow and down his neck, almost reaching his shoulders. But he was the closest thing Peter had to a friend. Of all the wretches on this ship, Peter thought, Eli is my best hope of finding a decent human response to my situation.

At the water's edge, they began casting nets for fish. "What did you do before you became a . . . pirate, Eli?" Peter asked.

"When I was a younger man, I was a carpenter," Eli replied. "Aye, I had me a little shop and a wife too. But when the war broke out between the English and the Frenchies, there was money to be made. Plenty of fellows outfitted ships and hired on men to rob the Spanish and French at sea. We were hailed as heroes then, for we were helping England."

"Why didn't you go back home when the war was over?" Peter asked.

The heavy-set man shrugged and said, "For one thing, my wife died, so there wasn't much to return to. And there's more money to be made at sea than at carpentering anyway."

"But pirating is against the law," Peter pointed out.

Eli shrugged again. "It doesn't seem like being a buccaneer is much different from being a war hero," he said. "I do the same thing I did during the war—sail the seas and collect booty."

The man and boy netted a slew of fat, silvery fish, and soon they were frying them over a fire built of driftwood.

As they ate the flaky white meat, Peter continued asking questions. He was trying to understand these strange men whose company fate had thrown him among.

"But how can you murder men for their goods?" he asked. "I saw one of the crew of my father's ship die from a cutlass wielded by a pirate. It was murder, like cutting a man down on the highway."

"I did not kill that poor swab," Eli said, wiping the grease from his chin with the back of his hand. "But I'm not saying I haven't done the same. Killing is a part of life, Peter. We do it in war, eh? This land we're standing on was taken from the Indians. They fought to keep what was theirs, and we killed them for it. How is it different, laddie?"

"The thought of murdering *any* man for *anything* is repugnant to me," Peter said.

"Ah, you are young, Peter. You will grow old fast enough on the *Infamy*, though," Eli said. "And who knows? You may grow to enjoy the pirate life. You can get rich at it. It's a good life, full of excitement and adventure. I would not trade this life for the carpenter's life I left behind."

Eli's round face split into a smile as he devoured his second fish. "We sail to the West Indies when the ship is heavy with gold," he said, spitting out a bone. "Let me tell you, it's a splendid life there indeed, laddie. We live on the beaches and lie in the sun. We eat pineapples and coconuts, and barbecue huge slabs of fresh meat. We eat until we can eat no more. Then we sleep and get up the next day and do it again."

Peter was just about to ask another question when he heard a shout.

"Horseman coming!" somebody yelled, and the pirates watched the dust of an oncoming horse.

Peter noticed that Eli Cooper's hand went to his pistol, and some of the others prepared to swing their cutlasses if the rider brought trouble.

When the horseman was still some distance away, Seth Hanes shouted, "State your business, stranger!"

The rider wore long trousers and a heavy dark coat. But long auburn curls spilled from under a wide-brimmed hat. "Where is Riley Oliver?" called a female voice.

"Ha!" Seth cried. " 'Tis a lass! A lass got up like a boy!"

Riley Oliver appeared then. "Caroline! I told you not to come unless you were in desperate trouble," he said. "What are you doing here?"

The girl dismounted from the horse and held the reins firmly. She looked around her with obvious disapproval and said, "Riley, when you wrote me that you had a crew and were sailing to the West Indies to trade in sugar and molasses, I thought you were in a respectable business. But look at these men! They are rabble! They look more like a pirate crew than seamen on a merchant ship."

Peter stared at the girl, at her creamy white skin and wide-set green eyes. What could such a lovely girl have to do with a vicious pirate like Oliver? he wondered.

Oliver ignored her comment. "I sent you money to open the millinery, Caroline. There was no reason for you to come here and meddle in my business," he said.

"Yes, there was," Caroline countered. "I have decided not to marry Samuel Reinholt. I despise the man."

"The wealthiest plantation owner in South Carolina and you despise him?" Oliver cried.

"Riley," Caroline said, "I won't marry a man for money."

"But you could live a life of leisure," Oliver insisted. " 'Tis as easy to love a rich man as a poor man. Reinholt is not a bad sort."

"When I marry, I want to marry a man who touches my heart," Caroline said. "So I have come to tell you that I shall not marry him. I wanted you to know since you are the only family I have."

Family? This must be Riley Oliver's sister! Peter realized. The man is supporting his sister with the proceeds from his vicious, illegal activities!

Caroline turned and looked at the pirates again, many of whom ogled her openly. "What a wretched lot your *sailors* are, Riley," she said.

Riley Oliver shifted uneasily. "It's not easy to get men to go to sea these days, Caroline. It's a hard life—and a dangerous one too. But the men work hard, and soon we shall be off to the West Indies."

Caroline's gaze settled on Peter then, and she raised her eyebrows. Just a trace of a smile touched her pretty face. "Now here's a fair-looking young man," she said.

Riley Oliver cast the boy a warning look that said, "If you dare say anything to her, I'll make sure you don't see the sun go down tonight." Peter could understand why the pirate wouldn't want his sister to know of his evil doings.

"That one?" Oliver replied casually. "That boy is a stupid lout. We brought him along to teach him the ropes, but he's as dense as an ox. He's seasick most of the time as well."

Caroline ignored her brother's words.

She walked toward Peter and said, "I don't believe a word of what my brother says. I imagine you are quite clever. What's your name, boy?"

Peter wasn't quite sure what Oliver would do if Peter blurted out the truth—that he was being held for ransom by a band of pirates led by her brother. Still, Peter surmised, it would only put the girl in jeopardy from the other pirates. They would be unwilling to let someone who knew their identities and location go. So he just said, "My name is Peter."

"I'm Caroline," the girl said. "I live in Charles Town. Where are you from?"

Peter hesitated. He almost said "Boston" but was afraid that she would continue to ask questions. And he wasn't sure how he would answer them without exposing her brother. So he said nothing.

"You're a silent one, aren't you?" Caroline laughed.

"I told you he is an ignorant lout," Oliver said. "Caroline, it is not good for you to be here. These are rough men who have not seen a woman in a long time. You mustn't come here again. Get back on your horse now. I will ride with you to the stage depot for your return home."

"I made it here by myself, and I shan't have any trouble returning," Caroline declared confidently. "I saw no perils along the way, and the distance is very short. The only disreputable sorts I've seen on this entire journey are your hirelings, Riley."

She climbed astride her horse and rode off before waiting for Oliver to catch and saddle one of the horses in the corral.

Most of the men returned to what they were doing—swilling grog or sleeping. But Peter noticed that Liam West was still staring hungrily at the girl as she rode away. The pirate stood licking his lips, almost trembling with excitement at the sight of the girl's beauty.

"Take care!" Oliver shouted after his sister.

"Take care yourself, Riley, that your wretched crew doesn't mutiny and throw you off the ship!" the girl shouted over her shoulder.

Peter smiled. He liked Caroline. She had a lot of spirit. He didn't know that

much about her, except that she had had a
hard life, a tough beginning. And yet she
had come through it with plenty of
gumption.

He glanced at Liam West, who was now
heading toward the corral. Riley Oliver
was walking off in another direction,
probably to join some companions over a
bottle of grog.

Nobody but Peter seemed to notice
West's movements. As Peter watched, he
saw West saddle a horse and climb onto
its back. Then quietly the man headed
down the beach in the direction Caroline
Oliver had gone.

4 "Eli," Peter said to the older man as he mended a net. "Did you see Liam West ride off just now?"

"Aye. And what of it? Thatcher lets us use the horses. And we give him a share of our booty," Eli said.

"Where do you think he was headed?" Peter asked.

"Who knows?" Eli replied. "A man who has been at sea a long time sometimes just wants the feel of horseflesh under him. Who knows what's in Liam West's mind? He's half-mad and mean as a cornered snake. I've seen him break a man's neck out of pure spite. But he's a good sailor."

"Eli, I think he plans to go after Riley Oliver's sister," Peter said.

Eli laughed and said, "Liam would not dare. Any man laying a hand on the girl would be fed to the sharks by Oliver."

"Maybe so, but I still think he rode out of here intending to do her harm," Peter said. "I'm going to warn Mr. Oliver."

Eli shrugged and said, "Suit yourself, boy. But if the two of them fight and Liam West wins, he'll come back here and kill you."

"But if Caroline comes to harm at the hands of Liam West, I'll never forgive myself," Peter said.

Peter found Riley Oliver with a group of men who were well on their way to getting drunk. "Mr. Oliver, sir," Peter began. "I fear Liam West has gone after your sister!"

Oliver halted his bottle halfway to his mouth. The young pirate turned then and looked at Peter. Then he looked in the direction Caroline had gone. Suddenly the implications of what Peter had said registered in his mind. Throwing down the bottle, he ran for the corral and leaped astride a jet-black horse. A few seconds later, he was riding at breakneck speed down the beach.

Peter returned to where Eli Cooper was working.

"You should have kept your mouth shut, laddie," Eli warned Peter. "There'll be trouble for sure."

"I could not let the girl come to harm," Peter said again, sure that he had done the right thing.

"She should not have come here," Eli

added, returning to fixing the net. "She took it upon herself to come here among these men. It can do you no good to get mixed up in it, Peter. She is not worth your life."

A little while later, Riley Oliver returned. With one arm he managed the horse. With the other he supported Caroline in front of him. She was leaning unsteadily to one side, and her arm was drenched in blood. She appeared to be unconscious.

Oliver climbed down and lifted his sister from the horse's back. He laid her gently on the beach, saying in a voice husky with emotion, "She tried to fight him off, and he slashed at her with the cutlass. I was almost too late."

He turned to Peter then and asked, "Can you find something to help her in your herb sack?"

"I'll try," Peter said.

As Eli went to get the herb sack from the ship, Peter knelt beside Caroline and carefully peeled the torn sleeve from her arm. The point of the cutlass had made a nasty wound, but it wasn't deep. Peter cleansed the wound with boiled water. Then, to stop the bleeding, he applied an agrimony compress. After about 30 minutes, the wound stopped bleeding, and Caroline opened her eyes. Her hand immediately went to her forehead, where there was a huge bump.

"What happened there?" her brother asked.

"I-I seem to remember falling off my horse when that man struck at me," Caroline explained groggily. "I must have hit my head on a rock."

Riley Oliver threw a questioning look at Peter, an obvious plea for help. Peter dug deeper into his sack and found what he was looking for. He steeped some flower heads and leaves in wine brought from the ship. Then he applied them to the bump. A few minutes later, the swelling started to go down.

"I tried to strike him with my whip," Caroline said, "but he came at me with his cutlass."

"Shhh," Oliver said. "Rest now, Caroline. You can tell us what happened later."

But his sister refused to be quiet. Her eyes swept over the men gathered in a circle around her. "Riley, what kind of men are you consorting with?" she asked. "The kind who chase a girl down and try to hurt her? In God's name, how do you defend sailing with such men?"

"Caroline, please," Oliver pleaded. "Be still. You need to rest."

But Caroline would not be silenced. "Where is this man who attacked me?" she demanded. "I want to give him a piece of my mind."

Her brother avoided her eyes.

"Riley?" Caroline pressed. "Where is he?"

Her brother sighed and said, "If you must know, he's dead. For what he tried to do to you, I have killed him. He will bother you no more, little sister."

A look of horror crossed Caroline's face. "Oh, Riley!" she cried. "What has happened to you? I don't even know you anymore." Her frightened eyes swept over the men again. "The only man here with an ounce of decency is this young man who is helping me." She gazed right at Peter then. "Thank you," she said.

"You're welcome," Peter mumbled, not looking up from his work.

Darkness was starting to descend, and they returned to the *Infamy* in the small boats. As Caroline was rowed out to the ship, it was obvious she was already feeling better.

"I don't know why I can't go back to Charles Town, Riley," she said. "I cannot leave the millinery shop to take care of itself. My ladies will be coming for the hats they ordered. Besides, I don't want to spend the night on this dirty ship among these horrid men."

"You need to rest after what you've been through," Oliver replied. He tried to sound gentle, but his eyes were brooding. Peter wondered what was going on in Oliver's mind. Was he undecided as to what to do with the son of the hated Edmund McCall, now that Peter had saved his sister? Or was he wrestling with what to tell Caroline about his livelihood? Or both?

Once on board, Caroline was put to bed in the captain's cabin. Oliver ordered Peter to stay at her bedside in case her condition worsened. A little while later, Oliver came in carrying a tray of food.

"Eat now, Caroline," he said. "You must regain your strength."

Caroline balked at the crude fare she was offered but eventually took a few bites.

"Dear sister," Oliver said in a heavy voice as he sat down beside her. "There are things that I must tell you that I dread speaking of."

"God forbid that my suspicions are true, Riley," Caroline said.

"I am a merchant—of sorts," her brother began.

"A merchant?" Caroline said. "So you buy and sell goods?"

"Well . . . yes," he replied, studying his hands in his lap.

"Riley, don't lie to me," Caroline said. "You know I've been able to see right through you since we were children. I don't believe you're a merchant. You are a buccaneer, a pirate. A common thief whose only difference from a highway robber is that you do your dirty work at sea!"

Oliver winced as if her harsh words caused him physical pain. "Caroline, we had nothing," he said. "We were destitute. Do you not remember? I wanted to set you up in business so you could support yourself. But that took money. I had no other means of getting it."

"Better that I should die of starvation than for you to condemn your soul for all eternity for being a pirate!" Caroline cried. Then she turned on Peter. "And you! Such a gentle, kind face. You were blessed with the gift of healing. And yet you cast your lot with these barbarous thieves!"

Peter started to speak to defend himself but then thought better of it. He wasn't sure what Oliver would want him to say.

Suddenly Caroline's eyes narrowed. "Riley," she said. "Why is this young man here? He doesn't act like the others, nor does he speak or dress like them."

Oliver sighed with resignation. "We kidnapped him from his father's ship headed for England," he admitted. "He is our prisoner."

Horror gripped Caroline then, and she turned her face toward the wall. "I refuse to listen!" she cried, covering her ears with her hands. "Would that I had died before hearing these monstrous things!"

Oliver left Caroline in the cabin then and motioned for Peter to follow.

"Captain Foster means to kill you once he receives the ransom," Oliver said in a flat voice. "That has been the plan from the beginning."

Peter felt a great sinking feeling within him. "But why?" he asked.

"You have lived among us," Oliver replied simply. "You know the coves we frequent. You know our weaknesses. You would be a great aid to those hunting us down to hang us."

"But why are you telling me this?" Peter asked.

"Because now I cannot let it happen. I am in your debt for the life of my sister," Oliver answered. "Except for your seeing Liam West follow her, she would now be dead—or worse."

"Will you let me return to Boston then?" Peter wanted to know.

"No," Oliver answered. "You could easily set the law on us before we have a chance to leave the coast. I'm taking you to the West Indies. Once there, you will be free to take a merchant ship back to Boston. Should you choose to turn us in at that time, we'll be too far away for them to come after us."

Later that day, Riley Oliver held a meeting of the crew. When they were all gathered on deck, he said, "I'm taking the *Infamy* and heading for the West Indies. There is plenty of gold and silver on board. We can divide it among ourselves now before I leave. Those who want to come with me can. Those who want to wait here for Captain Foster's return can do so."

"What about the ransom money the captain is bringing back?" Seth Hanes asked.

"Those men who choose to wait for Captain Foster will have fewer to share the ransom with," Oliver explained. "But those who come with me will get an equal share of any booty we take between here and the West Indies."

"The captain will be furious when he finds his ship gone," one of the men said.

"You can tell Captain Foster he'll find the *Infamy* docked safely in the West Indies if he wants it before we return to the colonies," Oliver said. "Tell him as well that he'll get a double share of any booty we take on at sea. That should cool his anger at our borrowing his ship."

After some more discussion, 18 men decided to join Riley Oliver. The others remained on shore to await Captain Foster and the ransom money.

The next morning at dawn, the *Infamy* sailed. Caroline and Peter were on board, as well as Seth Hanes, Josh Manley, and Eli Cooper.

"Caroline," Oliver told his sister, "I'll put you ashore in Charles Town tomorrow."

"And what of poor Peter?" Caroline asked crossly. "Surely he can come ashore with me. After all, you admitted you are holding him against his will."

Oliver shifted uneasily from one foot to the other under his sister's searing glance. "Caroline, Peter will run to the law and accuse me of piracy. I will be taken to Boston and hanged as others have been. Is that what you want to happen?"

"Then he is still a hostage?" Caroline demanded.

"I swear to you he shall be set free the moment we are safely in the West Indies," Oliver said. "I've already told him he can board a merchant ship and return to Boston whenever he wants. He will be free eventually. On my life, I promise that this will happen."

"I am ashamed of you, Riley Oliver," Caroline said.

"But—" Oliver started to argue.

"Peter," Caroline said, abruptly turning away from her brother, "will you walk on deck with me? I am feeling stronger now. And I would like to feel the clean salt air in my face—to sweep away the foul stench of this ship!"

Peter gave Caroline his arm, and they walked on the deck under bright blue skies.

"I'm sorry for what has happened to you, Peter," Caroline said. "And for the part my brother may have played."

"Don't worry about me," Peter replied. "After we drop anchor in the West Indies, I shall be going home. I simply must be patient a while longer."

"You may find this hard to believe, but we were once a respectable family," Caroline said sadly. "Our mother taught us from the Bible. And we sang hymns in church on the Sabbath."

"Your brother told me that your father was a tinsmith," Peter said. "He said that your father came on hard times and went to prison as a debtor." Peter shook his head and added, "That's not right. No man should go to prison for being poor."

"Yes," Caroline said. "I was very young when it happened, but I remember my father well. He was a good man with a cheerful outlook on life. He kept telling us better times were coming. But they never did."

Peter's heart ached as he wondered if Caroline knew the name of the man who had sent her father to debtors' prison. Had Oliver told her? If Oliver carried such a furnace of hatred in his soul against Edmund McCall, Peter reasoned, surely he had shared the man's name with Caroline.

"Caroline," Peter asked, "do you know the name of the man who sent your father to prison?'

Caroline was silent for a moment. She grasped the deck railing and stared into the rising sea waves. Finally she looked at Peter and said, "Yes, it was Edmund McCall. And Riley just told me that the man is your father."

5 "Don't worry, Peter. I don't blame you," Caroline assured him. "It happened long ago when you were a small boy. What say did you have in the business matters of your father? I want no part in vengeance against those who have wronged me, especially after seeing what it has done to my brother."

"It means a lot to me to hear you say that, Caroline," Peter said.

"And I hope you don't hold what Riley has done against me," Caroline went on. "I would gladly return to a life of poverty than see you in the clutches of these pirates."

"Don't give it a thought, Caroline. I hold no grudge against you," Peter said.

The next day, as promised, Oliver docked in Charles Town. Peter was on deck to see Caroline off.

"Good-bye, Caroline," he said. "I'm glad we had the chance to meet—even if it wasn't under the best of circumstances."

"And I'm glad too," Caroline replied. She started to walk away but then stopped. "Peter, I never asked you. Why were you on that ship headed for England?"

"I was on my way to Cambridge

University," Peter replied. "It's my parents' hope that I get a good education, better than I can get in Boston."

"What will you study at Cambridge?" the girl asked.

"I intend to become a doctor," Peter stated with certainty. He realized he was discussing his future again. For a few, terrible days, he had doubted that he had a future. Now it felt good to be planning for it again.

"You will make a fine doctor," Caroline declared. Then she turned in a circle in front of him. "Look how I have benefited from your skills."

"You do look better than when your brother brought you back to the beach," Peter conceded modestly.

"Of course I do," the girl replied. "And I'm getting better every moment." Then she did something that surprised Peter. She reached up and kissed him on the cheek. "Take care, Peter McCall," she said. "And visit me if you're ever in Charles Town."

Peter nodded and replied, "I am eager to do so."

Oliver came up then and led his sister off

the ship and into a stagecoach on the dock. A few minutes later, he returned to the *Infamy* and yelled, "Cast off, men!"

The *Infamy* was soon underway again, heading south toward the West Indies. It was a beautiful, sunny day, with just enough wind to fill the sails. Peter stood on deck, gazing at the vast expanse of ocean all around him. He wondered with anxiety when they might spot another ship. He realized that any merchant ship that came into the path of the schooner faced certain ambush. Peter hoped desperately that the *Infamy* would find no easy prey. The thought of Riley Oliver leading his rampaging pirates onto another victim ship terrified him. Peter didn't want to see more men die. And he did not want to see Oliver partake in any more illegal activities. Peter did not want to feel obligated to testify against him if he ever came before an Admiralty Court. He did not want to play a part in hanging Caroline's brother.

Peter approached Riley Oliver then and said, "Surely you don't intend to spend your life in this foul business?"

"No. I just need a bit more of a fortune," Oliver replied. "Then I shall retire as a gentleman. I'll grow fruit and flowers from the West Indies. And I'll have a hothouse when the weather grows too cold. My gardens will be the talk of Charles Town."

"I had hoped you'd had enough of the bloody business," Peter remarked.

Oliver smiled at the boy. "Almost, but not quite," he said. "But I swear to you I will kill no one unless it's absolutely necessary. And that you shall be free when we drop anchor in the West Indies. You saved the life of my sister. For that I shall keep my word to free you at whatever the cost."

"Oliver, I will not join in your devilish deeds," Peter warned.

"I thought we might yet make a buccaneer out of you," Oliver chuckled. "But since we haven't, you may stay below while we're about our business. I am so generous that even though you do not help us collect booty, you may have a share of it—just for the trouble I've put you through."

Josh Manley was standing nearby and

heard Oliver's grand gesture. "He deserves no share," Josh said sullenly, throwing a piercing glare Peter's way.

"Don't worry, Manley," Oliver laughed, slapping the man on the back. "There will be plenty for all. The way between here and the Indies is littered with merchant ships."

He walked away then, but Josh Manley continued to stare hatefully at Peter. The boy squirmed uneasily under the pirate's glare. Finally Peter said, "I want no reward from your bloody crimes, Manley."

"That's what you say now," Manley retorted. "But once you get a look at the gold, you'll change your mind." He stalked away then, throwing a warning glance over his shoulder.

The thought of a pirate like Manley hating him made Peter shudder. He told himself that from now on he'd watch his back when Manley was around.

As evening fell, the waves grew choppy, pitching the ship about. The clouds gathered and darkened, bringing a squall with them. As Peter stood on the deck watching the gathering storm, the *Infamy* suddenly leaped on the crest of a great wave. Water splashed on the deck, catching Peter by surprise. He almost slipped and fell.

The canvas of the sails billowed in the howling wind, and the bowsprit twisted like a serpent.

"Heave lively now!" Riley Oliver shouted as the men scrambled over the footropes, the sails blowing over them. The ship was climbing mountainous waves now.

Peter stared at the rope rigging. First it would stretch taut. Then it would go slack and seem to come undone. He wondered what was wrong with it.

"Maybe we'll all drown like rats, laddie," Eli laughed, seeing the worry on the boy's face. He was obviously amused at Peter's lack of understanding of how the rigging worked.

Peter had never been so sick. He hung on to the bulwarks for his life as the *Infamy* became a bucking stallion.

Josh Manley seemed to materialize at Peter's side from out of the spray. Josh had been securing the sails, but now he sneered at Peter, nearly green with seasickness, clinging to the slippery deck. "Looks like you might be going over the edge soon," Josh whispered in a taunting voice.

Peter was too out of breath from holding on to reply. Josh suddenly gave him a mighty shove toward the railing of the ship. Peter barely caught himself before going overboard. In the darkness of the storm and the night, he saw Josh throw back his head and laugh, his one eye gleaming with devilish amusement. Then as mysteriously as he had come, Josh disappeared.

He tried to kill me, Peter realized with horror. But why is that so shocking? he thought. These men are criminals. Some of them are worse than others, but they're all willing to rob, plunder, and kill. Even Riley Oliver with his sweet sister could kill without regret. Hadn't he dispatched Liam West without a backward glance? True, he had good reason, but still he did the deed with such chilling ease. Life means nothing to these men. If Josh's sinister little joke had worked, he would have recalled it as no more significant than drowning a rat.

"Your first bad storm, eh, laddie?" Eli asked later when the storm subsided. "You look like you've seen a ghost. I don't blame you. Many a man's been lost in these squalls."

Peter knew it would do no good and might well do harm if he mentioned what Josh had tried to do. So he nodded and said, "I was on the Atlantic once with my father, and we went through a storm. But it was nothing like this one, and we were not far from land."

"You were lucky then," Eli said. "The Atlantic storms can be fierce ones. The sea is a wicked witch when she's angry."

"I don't understand why anyone would be willing to live with such danger all the time," Peter remarked.

"Ah, well, the sea gets in your blood," Eli replied. "I'll die aboard a ship most likely. I hope it comes quick when it's my turn. I wouldn't like to catch a sickness and linger. I've seen men whose death is a long, drawn-out affair, and I've seen men hanged. I'd rather be hanged than to spend many months at dying."

Peter said nothing. He knew Eli was troubled by stomach pains. Perhaps the pirate feared these pains were the start of some fatal illness.

"I have heard that there are sometimes pardons for pirates if they pledge to give up the business," Peter said.

"Aye," Eli said, nodding, "if they pledge to live honorable lives. But that is not for me. I could not live ashore for long. My blood has turned to sea water. I would flop on dry land like a hooked fish gasping for air."

Oliver came walking down the deck then, surveying the damage from the storm. Eli asked, "How about you, Oliver? Could you give up life on the high seas? Could you take a pardon from the king and be a butcher or a baker somewhere?"

"I would give it up if I had enough wealth to own a house with Chippendale furniture and Chinese wallpaper," Oliver laughed.

"Ah," Eli said, smiling grimly. "Then let us hope for a fat ship loaded with valuable cargo to come our way. Then you shall have your prized house."

The talk of the two men made Peter long even more to be off the ship before more bloodshed occurred. Peter gazed at the sea around him and wondered how far they were from land. Then he sighed. It wouldn't matter, he thought. I'm not a very good swimmer and would drown before I went half a mile.

He thought about his parents then and how worried they must be. His mother especially. She had never experienced any real misfortune that Peter could remember. Her four daughters were healthy and settled into good lives. There were always minor things to contend with, bouts of influenza, broken bones, colds. And the year of the terrible smallpox outbreak, 1752, had left one of the girls with a minor disfigurement. But none of that could have prepared her for what had happened to Peter. *And* not knowing if he were alive or dead.

Peter knew that by now his father had paid the ransom. Whatever amount

Captain Foster asked for, Edmund McCall would pay. Poor Father, Peter thought. He's probably waiting to hear that I have been freed. And in the meantime, Captain Foster is hurrying back to the South Carolina coastal cove to put an end to me!

* * *

The moment Peter dreaded came three days later. Cloaked by morning fog, the crew of the *Infamy* watched in silence as a merchant ship floated by.

"The prize of a lifetime," Riley Oliver whispered in awe. "On her way to the Indies with a cargo of hemp, Barcelona silks, and barrels of molasses, I'll wager."

Peter's heart sank. "Oliver, you cannot murder those men for their goods," he insisted.

"Don't worry, boy. If the captain of the vessel surrenders the cargo, I'll not harm the hair of any man's head," the young pirate promised.

You might not, Peter thought, but what about the others? He knew for certain that Josh Manley would kill anyone who got in his way. And many of the others would do the same.

As the ship neared the spot where the *Infamy* waited, all the pirates stood ready to clamber aboard. With a blast from the pirate ship's guns, the ambush was underway. A huge fountain of water arose before the merchant ship where the guns had churned the seas.

As the two ships neared each other, Peter could read the name of the other ship—the *Expedition*. They were so close now that he could see the terror in the eyes of the sailors on board the merchant ship. Peter felt sorry for the captain of the *Expedition*. The white-haired man stood trembling on the deck as he watched the horde of cutthroats bounding toward his ship.

6 Peter was just about to go below deck when he saw with relief that the captain of the other ship was surrendering without a fight.

" 'Tis no use fighting," Peter heard him call to his crew. "We're far outnumbered."

Immediately the pirates swarmed aboard the *Expedition*.

"Bring the cargo on deck!" Riley Oliver ordered. The captain told his men to do as they were told. Several pirates, weapons in hand, accompanied the sailors to the hold below the ship. A few minutes later, crates of cargo were set on the deck for Oliver's inspection.

The ship turned out to be even richer than expected. It carried not only a fat load of valuable goods, but gold and silver as well. With the help of the sailors of the other boat, the pirates transferred the cargo and the treasure to the *Infamy*. It was the middle of the afternoon when the buccaneers finally sailed off with their booty, leaving the merchant ship empty but unharmed.

"You have brought us luck, Peter

McCall!" Oliver shouted in high spirits when the *Infamy* got underway.

Josh Manley stepped forward then, his one eye staring balefully at Oliver. "How is the treasure to be divided?" he demanded to know.

"Captain Foster will get part of it," Oliver said. "He is still captain of this borrowed ship, and therefore, we must reserve two shares for him. As for the rest, we shall have one share apiece."

"Captain Foster is a scoundrel and a cheat," Josh Manley declared. "Sooner or later, he'd have stirred up disputes among us over the ransom money. He likes nothing better than to have us kill each other off. Then we lessen the number of men to share the loot. He deserves no share. And you, Riley Oliver, should not be captain. It is a position I should have."

Oliver placed his hands on his hips belligerently and said, "The crew voted that I should take Foster's place when we left the cove."

"I disremember a fair vote," Josh snarled. "You took command and decided to make orders that I cannot abide."

"Then let us decide who is to be captain in a duel," Oliver challenged.

"Agreed," Josh said.

Seth Hanes stepped forward then. "You remember what the captain said, Oliver. No fighting aboard ship."

"Then we'll put ashore on the next deserted isle," Oliver replied. "The man who returns to the ship still able to stand—or still alive—shall be her captain."

"I'll take Seth Hanes with me to make sure the duel is kept fair," Josh said.

"And I will take young Peter, the herbalist," Oliver said. "For he can treat what wounds we may inflict—if they are not fatal."

"No herbalist shall be able to cure you when I am done," Josh boasted. He stalked away then and returned to his work on the sails.

When Peter could speak to Oliver alone, he said, "Are you mad?"

Oliver laughed. "I am by far the better duelist," he said. "I shall dispatch him easily enough. Have no fear, Peter. We shall leave Josh Manley on the island. And good riddance to him too! I have always felt the need to guard my back when he is around."

And if you don't win, Peter thought as Oliver walked away, what will become of me? Will they kill me? Or will they force me into their service? Causing me to spend the rest of my life sailing the seas, robbing and looting innocent victims? Peter didn't know which was worse.

The ship sailed on a fresh wind for more than two hours before coming upon a deserted island. It was a small patch of land in the midst of the blue-green sea. From the deck of the *Infamy*, Peter could see clumps of green palm trees and gently sloping, white beaches.

This island is unspoiled by humans, Peter thought, shaking his head. A natural paradise. And now it will be the scene of a gruesome battle.

Peter climbed into a rowboat with the three pirates. A tenseness pervaded the small boat, and no one spoke as they made their way to the island. Glancing over his shoulder, Peter could see the buccaneers lined up on deck, waiting to watch the battle.

When they reached the island, Seth Hanes tied the boat to a tree. Peter carried his sack of herbs and the iron box containing the two dueling pistols the men would use.

Riley Oliver and Josh Manley removed their coats. Then they took their places, back-to-back on the beach.

"You know the rules," Seth Hanes said. "Each man is to take ten steps, then turn and fire."

"You count off, Hanes," Oliver said.

"One . . . two . . . three . . . four . . . five . . ." Seth called out as the two men separated and headed in opposite directions.

"Six . . . seven . . . eight . . . nine . . . ten!"

Peter watched in horror as the men turned and fired. Both men remained standing, but Josh Manley's pistol went flying from his hand. He clutched his shoulder in pain. Oliver's bullet had entered Manley's shoulder just a few inches above his heart! Oliver, though, was unharmed.

Suddenly Manley grabbed his cutlass in his good hand, swinging it like the blades of a windmill. "I'll best you with this, Oliver!" he shrieked.

It would have been a simple matter for Oliver to fire again and finish off his opponent. But instead the young pirate threw down his pistol and brandished his own cutlass. "Let no man claim I didn't fight fair!" he shouted.

The silence of the island was instantly replaced with the crashing of steel. For a quarter of an hour, the two men fought, each trying desperately to make a deadly thrust at the other. Peter could hear bloodthirsty shouts and cheers coming from the deck of the *Infamy*.

"Drive the blade home, Manley!" one pirate yelled.

"Kill the scoundrel, Oliver!" another shouted.

Finally Riley Oliver slashed into Josh Manley's good shoulder, rendering the other man helpless. Manley collapsed onto the sand, where he lay looking up beseechingly at his foe. In horror Peter watched as Oliver raised his cutlass for the final blow.

"Take his head!" the crew yelled from the boat. "Kill him! Kill him! Kill him!"

Suddenly Peter heard an explosion, and young Riley Oliver crumpled to the sand in a heap.

Confused, Peter turned and looked at Seth Hanes. In his hand, Hanes held Oliver's dueling pistol, still smoking. He glanced at Peter and then looked away again. It was obvious he was unconcerned with the boy's presence. Hanes approached the spot where Oliver had fallen. He reached down and picked up the cutlass that lay a few inches from Oliver's hand. Now Hanes raised the cutlass for the final blow.

Suddenly Peter thought of Caroline. She loved Oliver, despite his faults. And if he were killed, she would be alone in the world. I can't let that happen, Peter thought. I've got to help him for her sake.

Desperate to do something, he lunged at Hanes, knocking him off his feet. The cutlass flew from Hanes' hand and landed several feet away. Peter had taken the older man off guard, and for a few seconds he had the advantage. But Seth Hanes was heavier and a more experienced fighter than Peter. He soon turned the advantage around. Just as Hanes was about to pin Peter to the ground, Peter spotted a knife in Seth's belt. Peter yanked out the knife and blindly struck at the other man's midsection. With a heavy groan, Hanes tumbled backward. The sand around him was soon soaked with blood.

Peter staggered to his feet, sick and stunned. What had he done? The pirate was not moving! A knife was sticking out of his stomach—the knife Peter had put there! Peter felt a wave of nausea come over him. And before he knew it, he was on his knees, retching onto the sand.

"So we've made a buccaneer out of you after all, eh?" a voice from behind him said.

Peter turned to see Josh Manley on his feet, swaying unsteadily. Blood was dripping freely from his wounds.

"He . . . he shot Oliver in the back," Peter tried to explain.

"No matter. All that matters is that I am now captain of the *Infamy*," Manley said smugly, nodding toward Oliver's still form. "Now get in the boat and get us back to the ship. And don't forget your herb sack. Looks like I'll be needing your services after all."

Manley headed toward the rowboat, but Peter remained where he was. He glanced at Oliver's still form on the beach. He felt a sinking feeling as he realized that Oliver was probably dead.

Peter shook his head in despair. What he had dreaded most had happened. Oliver had lost, and Peter was to be forced into service by these villains. He saw his future dissolving before him. Now instead of becoming a doctor, he would become a pirate, a criminal with a price on his head. And it wouldn't matter that he had been forced into it. If he was caught, he would hang with the rest of them.

"Move!" Manley barked. "We sail within the hour. And you'll be taking over Seth Hanes' duties—permanently!"

I can't do it, Peter told himself. I *won't*

do it! I don't know what I'll do, but I'll not let my life take this disastrous course.

"No!" he shouted. "I'll not become a thief and a murderer!"

"You'll become whatever I want you to become!" Manley seethed.

Peter looked wildly around him. Could he sustain himself on this tiny island? he wondered.

But Josh Manley read his thoughts. "Don't bother thinking you can stay here, laddie," he warned. "There's nothing to eat on this island but a few berries. More than likely, there's no life here at all. And no fresh water to be had either. You can't drink sea water, you know! We're outside the shipping lanes, and you'll perish long before another boat gets here!"

Then Peter remembered the rowboat. Perhaps he could escape in it, he thought.

But again Josh knew what he was thinking. He laughed and said, "Hah! Your puny arms are no match for the power of the *Infamy*!"

Peter knew Josh was right. The ship would run him down and kill him before he got a mile away. He decided that his only chance was to try to survive on the island until another ship came along. He wheeled then and started running up a small bluff toward some palm trees.

"Come back!" Josh Manley yelled. "You'll starve here!"

He made an effort to follow the boy, but Peter knew there was no way Josh could catch him. The man was weakening from a loss of blood. Peter quickly outdistanced him and took refuge in the stand of palm trees.

Manley stopped on the beach and turned back toward the rowboat. "The devil take you then!" he shouted over his shoulder. "The next ship that comes this way will find your bones on the beach— years from now!"

7 Peter watched as the pirate climbed into the small boat and slowly made his way back to the schooner. The boy felt panic begin to overtake him as he stood there. What had he done? He was alone on an island with two dead men! His father had told him stories of marooned sailors going mad from thirst and starvation. Would that be his fate if he stayed there? he wondered.

I can still stop him, he thought. If I go with him, at least I'll live. Peter opened his mouth to yell, but the words stuck in his throat. Killing Seth Hanes had sickened him beyond belief—and that had been in self-defense! How could he ever kill innocent men? He shook his head then and knew he had made the right decision. Better to take my chances on the island than to commit myself to a life of piracy, he told himself again.

Now Peter walked back to where the two pirates lay. There was Seth Hanes, grotesque in death, his lips still twisted in his last curses. His body was close to the water. So Peter knew that before long the tide would take him to his watery grave.

Peter hurried toward Riley Oliver then.

"Peter," Oliver mumbled as the boy turned him over.

"You're alive!" Peter gasped.

"Not for long," Oliver whispered. "The ball in me is burning like fire."

Peter could see a gaping hole in Oliver's side just above his waist. A thought came to Peter, a distasteful, frightening thought, yet one laced with hope. If no vital organs had been hit, Oliver might live—if the ball was removed. Then Peter would not be alone on the island.

But could he cut the steel ball from the injured man? he wondered. He sighed then and shook his head. He had never done anything like that. It was one thing to collect dried leaves and flower blossoms to ease a bellyache or soothe a cut. But to find a flintlock ball and remove it from a human body . . .

"They marooned us, eh?" Oliver said in a weak voice. "The lot of them is not worth a stone, the infernal devils. "

"Be quiet and save your strength," Peter said.

But Oliver's eyes had already closed,

and his head had dropped to one side. Peter knew that he was unconscious.

He found Oliver's knife in his belt and tested the blade against his thumb. It was certainly sharp enough. Then he looked at the wound again. The opening was already starting to shrink. If the wound closed over on the outside, it would fester on the inside. The infection would spread throughout Oliver's body then, and he would surely die.

Peter knew that the sooner he went after the ball, the easier it would be. And this was the time to do it—when Oliver was unconscious and would feel no pain.

He took a deep breath and peeled the shirt away from the injured area. Fighting waves of nausea, he gingerly inserted the tip of the knife into the wound. Immediately, blood streamed out around Peter's hands. He closed his eyes to block out the sight and slowly pressed the blade in farther until he felt it touch the metal ball. Then he worked the tip of the blade around the back of the ball and, with a firm pressure, eased the ball out.

Soaked in sweat, Peter lay down on the

beach. He was panting and close to tears. Nothing had prepared him for what he had just done. He gave himself a few minutes to recover before going on. When his breathing was normal again, he got up and found his herb sack, glad now that Oliver had insisted he bring it.

His next job, he knew, was to clean the wound to prevent infection. But for that he would need a fire.

He had seen his grandfather once start a fire by striking steel against a rock, creating sparks. The sparks, in turn, ignited tinder made out of dried tree bark.

Peter glanced around the beach. His eyes fell upon Oliver's cutlass, still lying in the sand. That will do, he thought. But when he went to recover the cutlass, the body of Seth Hanes caught his eye. And it reminded him that the tide would be coming in later. He decided to move to higher ground before building the fire. That way he could keep it going in case he needed it again. And he wouldn't have to worry about the fire being drowned out.

With much effort, he dragged the unconscious Riley Oliver up the small bluff to the grove of palm trees he had hidden in earlier.

After resting a few minutes, he gathered several pieces of old tree bark and shredded it fine with his fingers. He laid the tinder next to a nearby rock. Then he struck the long blade of the cutlass against the rock, allowing the sparks to fall on the tinder. After several tries, a tongue of flame rose from the tinder. Carefully he fanned the flame with a palm leaf and soon had a small fire going. To this he added more tree bark and dried leaves. After about 15 minutes, the fire was burning nicely. Peter walked the beach looking for driftwood. It took him a long time, but finally he found several small pieces. He added some of these to the fire and set the rest aside for later.

He opened his herb sack and removed a small pot from it. Then he filled the pot with water and boiled the water. After the water had cooled some, he made a poultice of agrimony and cleansed Oliver's wound. He covered the wound with a clean rag from his sack. Then he took off his shirt and tied it around Oliver's middle to hold the rag in place.

Exhausted, he threw himself down beside Oliver and tried to sleep. But every time he was close to drifting off, the image of Seth Hanes with a knife in his stomach jerked him awake again. Had he actually killed a man? he wondered. Perhaps it had not really happened. Perhaps it had just been a dream. He hoped against hope that that was true. Finally, full of dread, he sat up and peered toward the beach. There was Hanes' body, waiting patiently for the tide to take it away. So he really had taken another man's life.

Peter sighed sadly. What would my parents think of their only son now? he wondered. They sent me to school to learn how to save lives, and instead I've taken one.

He glanced at Oliver then and moved over to feel his forehead. It was feverish, as if infection had already set in. It's no wonder in such a hot, sultry climate, Peter thought. The combination of heat and moisture, his grandfather always said, was the perfect breeding ground for fever. He looked at Oliver's face then. It was clammy and the color of paste. Peter longed to give him a drink of water, but he had none to give. Without water, Oliver's body would become dehydrated and then . . .

With profound sadness, Peter realized that despite his efforts to save him, the young man beside him could easily die.

And I will die too, he thought. Without food, without water, and with no ships coming this way for who knows how long. With only those vicious pirates knowing I'm here. What chance do I have?

For the first time since he had been kidnapped, Peter came close to losing hope completely. For the first time since the ordeal had begun, he was certain that he would die.

8 When Peter awoke again, night had fallen on the island. He checked Oliver's forehead and noted that it was still warm. He tore a scrap off the shirt he had wrapped around Oliver. Then he soaked the cloth in water and laid it across the injured man's forehead. He hoped the coolness of the cloth would alleviate the fever somewhat.

He added another piece of driftwood to the fire to keep it from going out. Then, feeling at a loss to do anything more for Oliver, he took a walk down the beach. He noticed with relief that Seth Hanes' body was finally gone, washed away by the evening tide.

"May you rest in peace, Seth Hanes," Peter said aloud as he gazed out over the water. He hadn't liked the pirate. But he felt obliged to say something over the man's death since he himself had been the cause of it.

Overhead, stars sparkled clear in the warm tropical night, and the moon cast a soft, ivory reflection on the water. Peter's mind vaulted back to night strolls along Boston harbor with his grandfather.

Besides being an herbalist, Abraham McCall had been an amateur astronomer. And he had willingly shared his knowledge of the heavens with Peter. On their walks, he would fill the boy's head with stories of Greek gods and goddesses immortalized in the constellations.

Peter remembered the crabs playing in the harbor when the tide went out. He wondered if there were crabs here. That would be something to catch and eat anyway, he thought as he felt the gnaw of hunger pangs. He made up his mind to look in the morning.

A slight wind rustled the palm trees overhead. Peter glanced up and was surprised to see something moving through the tops of the fronds. In the moonlight it looked like a child! It had arms and legs and now and then stood upright. Suddenly Peter realized what it was—a monkey! He was surprised because Josh Manley had said there was probably no life on the island.

Then Peter remembered something his grandfather had told him. Sometimes during storms, wildlife was brought to an island by trees that were washed up on the beach. Maybe many years ago a family of monkeys had arrived by clinging to the trunk of an uprooted tree. If there were monkeys, perhaps there were other animals too. And if there are animals, it only follows that there are probably edible plants, Peter thought with hope rising in his heart.

Peter stared as the frisky monkey leaped gracefully to the next tree. He wondered what monkeys tasted like. He shuddered at the thought of eating a monkey. How would he get one anyway? he asked himself.

But then Peter wondered, What do these monkeys eat? It was then that he saw what looked like bunches of coconuts hanging at the tops of the trees. He squinted his eyes and peered up through the darkness. There *were* coconuts up there. He was sure of it! Somehow coconut palms had taken root on the island. Peter knew that coconuts were actually seeds. Perhaps one had been transported during a storm, and the tide had planted it.

Peter's heart raced with excitement. Coconuts would be good to eat. The milk inside the fruit was supposed to be delicious, and it would substitute for water! As soon as it was light, he would figure out some way to get those coconuts down, he decided.

Peter returned to Riley Oliver then and found him groaning restlessly. Was the infection worsening? he wondered with dread.

He felt a sudden surge of hatred for the pirates who had marooned them. They were wicked men with no sense of conscience. Even Eli Cooper, whom Peter had considered a friend, had obviously made no move to prevent their being left behind.

The year before, Peter's father had seen two pirates named Samuel Parkes and Benjamin Hawks hanged in Boston. He had told Peter that he and other Bostonians were doing their civic duty by turning out to watch two criminals justly punished. At the time, Peter had felt sorry for Parkes and Hawks as he pictured their lifeless bodies swinging from the gallows.

But now he thought he would feel little sympathy for them. Piracy was an evil business. And any punishment pirates received was certainly their due.

Peter was exhausted and felt the need for more sleep, but he decided to check Oliver's wound first. The moon was high in the sky now and provided him with enough light to see. Carefully he removed the coverings, exposing the bullet hole. His heart sank when he saw a dark area all around the wound—the spreading red of infection. Peter sighed. The wound would have to be cleaned again before it got any worse.

He stoked the fire with the rest of the driftwood and boiled more water. Then he added more agrimony from his sack. He tore additional rags from the legs of his trousers and dipped them into the hot mixture. Then he held them against the wound. Over and over he applied hot poultices to the wound, trying to drive away the infection. He rushed back and forth, keeping the fire going and heating more seawater for most of the night.

Finally, fatigued past the point of

thinking, he covered the wound again and lay back on the sand. He didn't know whether Oliver would live or die, but he felt he had done all he could for now. He fell asleep thinking he would check on Oliver again in the morning to see if his efforts had paid off.

* * *

With the dawn glowing pink and sea birds shrieking overhead, Peter awakened. For a minute he didn't know where he was. Then it came to him that he was marooned on a tropical island with a dying pirate.

"Did you have yourself a good sleep, laddie?" said a nearby voice.

Peter turned his head to see Riley Oliver sitting against a palm tree a few feet away. "Oliver!" he cried. "You're alive!"

"Unless the devil came for me during the night and left you a ghost for a companion," Oliver chuckled.

"Let me take a look at that wound," Peter said. He removed the covering and inspected the wound. The red glow of infection was nearly gone!

"The hot poultices worked!" he exclaimed in amazement, his spirits suddenly rising. Oliver was out of danger! He couldn't believe he had actually been instrumental in saving a person's life. The feeling he got from knowing that was exhilarating. If he'd had any doubts about becoming a doctor before, they were gone now. He *would* get off this island, and he *would* go into medicine, he told himself. The world needed him. It was awaiting what he had to offer. And he would offer it his best!

"Hot poultices? Being marooned has made you daft already," Oliver said. "Where would you get hot poultices when you have no fire?"

"I made one using sparks from your cutlass and a rock," Peter explained. He nodded at a pile of smoldering ashes a few feet away, the only thing that remained of the fire from the night before.

"You are a wonder, lad!" Oliver exclaimed. "You have saved my sister's life and now mine. I am in debt to you, Peter McCall."

"My pleasure!" Peter said, smiling.

Oliver grew serious then. "Can you ever forgive me, lad, for kidnapping you from your father's ship?" he asked.

"I'll forgive you on one condition," Peter offered. "That you forgive my father."

Oliver scowled at the suggestion.

"I'm not excusing my father," Peter said quickly. "But I've been giving it some thought. I doubt he was aware of the misery he caused your family. He has men working for him, men who handle his business affairs. It's very likely that he never even saw your father's request to postpone payment of the interest."

Oliver looked unconvinced.

"He's not a bad sort of fellow. I swear he's not," Peter pressed. "Can you forgive him?"

Oliver sighed. "Aye, you're probably right," he admitted. "Edmund McCall is probably no more of a scoundrel than I am. I'll try to think softer of him from now on."

"That's close enough," Peter smiled.

9 Peter spent an hour walking the island, gathering more driftwood. He wanted to keep the fire going in case they were able to get fish or crab to eat.

As he returned with his armload of wood, he remembered the coconuts and looked up. He was shocked. The trees were taller than they had looked the night before by moonlight. They were at least 75 feet tall!

"I saw monkeys in those trees last night," he said to Oliver. "They must be eating the coconuts."

"Aye, they probably are," Oliver agreed.

"Do you think I could bring down one of those coconuts with a slingshot—provided I could make one, that is?" Peter asked.

Oliver smiled. "Not with a slingshot, laddie. Coconuts are bound too tightly to a tree. If you want one of those nuts, you'll either have to wait for it to fall or climb the tree and cut it down with a knife."

Peter stared up at the trees. They seemed to reach the very heavens. "But how could I climb trees such as those?" he asked. "They're straight up, and their bark looks so smooth. They have no branches to use as stepping stones."

"You'll have to make a sling to fasten around your waist. It'll catch you if you slip," Oliver replied. "Then you make your way up, gripping with both your hands and your feet."

Peter looked up at the treetops again. He didn't much relish the idea of climbing that high. But water was essential to keeping the two of them alive, and he knew he had no choice.

Peter set to work making a sling. Under Oliver's direction, he fashioned it out of their shirts. Then he tied it at his waist, looping it around the tree trunk first. After tugging at it a few times to make sure it was secure, he was ready.

"Here's my knife," Oliver said, standing up and limping over to him. "Hold it in your teeth so your hands are free."

Peter took the knife and began climbing, easing the sling up as he went. He was surprised at how rough the bark felt against his bare feet and hands. It had looked so smooth before.

"Don't look down," Oliver called from

below. "Keep your eyes on the coconuts. And lean back into the sling. It will give you support."

Peter tried to do as Oliver said. But suddenly, when he was only about 25 feet above the ground, the palm tree wavered in the wind. Peter had the giddy sensation of clinging to the rigging of a ship during a storm. He gasped and grasped the trunk tightly. The knife dropped from his teeth, and Peter watched it fall to the sand below.

"Are you all right?" Oliver called.

Peter peered down at Oliver. Already the pirate looked as if he were no bigger than an ant. Peter knew he couldn't go up any higher. The rope sling had slackened when he grasped the tree, and he was now holding on with his strength alone.

Oliver cupped his hands and called out, "Lean back into the sling, Peter!"

But Peter could not let go of his hold on the trunk. If he did, he might slip. And he couldn't risk falling and breaking a leg. Slowly he edged his way down the palm tree. It seemed to take forever. With every move, he scraped his hands and feet and even his face. He was thankful when he finally felt the ground beneath him.

"I'm sorry, Oliver," he apologized, rubbing the raw palms of his hands. "I just froze."

"Ah, well, laddie," Oliver said, limping over to a nearby rock. "You can try again later. In the meantime, perhaps we can find another source of water—one that's within our reach."

He flipped the rock over and picked up something from the ground. Then he held aloft a wriggling insect. "The Good Book tells us that John the Baptist ate insects along with honey," Oliver said. "If they're good enough for him, they're good enough for me!"

With that, he popped the insect into his mouth and chewed noisily. "Ah," he said, smacking his lips. "Already my parched throat feels better!"

The boy shuddered, bringing a roar of laughter from Oliver. "When you're a pirate, laddie, you learn to eat whatever you have to in order to survive!" he said.

Peter picked up the knife and turned back to the palm tree. He'd heard of people eating insects to survive. But he wasn't going to be one of them. He'd risk heights over eating bugs any day, he decided.

He started up the tree once more, knife in his teeth. This time he did everything he was supposed to do. Once he slipped about a foot, but, as Oliver had said, the sling caught him.

"You're doing fine!" Oliver called from below. Already his voice sounded far away. But Peter did not look down. He continued inching his way up the trunk, moving the sling as he went.

After a few minutes, he stopped to rest. He was sweating profusely from his efforts. He leaned back against the sling and gazed into the treetops around him, being careful not to look down. He was surprised to see that he was being watched—by several pairs of eyes! Then he remembered the monkeys he had seen the night before. They were peering out at him now from behind palm fronds.

He removed the knife from his teeth and yelled, "Scat or I'll eat you!"

In an instant the monkeys were gone,

chattering and jumping from tree to tree until they were out of sight.

Peter laughed and continued on his way. A few minutes later, he reached the coconuts. He edged himself around the trunk until he was next to a cluster of several nuts. Then he reached up and slashed at them with the knife. Slowly he cut through the fibers that held the nuts to the tree. The coconuts fell heavily to the sand below.

Oliver cheered as Peter painstakingly made his way back down. His hands and feet were bleeding, and he felt as if he had just climbed a huge mountain. "Good job, my boy!" Oliver exclaimed when Peter reached the ground.

"Thanks," Peter said. He walked around then, gathering his prizes. "Some of them are green," he said in disappointment. "They aren't ripe!"

"All the better," Oliver replied. "That kind is full of milk. Milk to slake the thirst!"

Peter picked up a green coconut and shook it. "You're right. I can hear the milk sloshing around in there."

"Hammer a hole into the shell with the blade of my knife, Peter, and be careful not to spill any. I've got a thirst as big as the ocean!" Oliver said.

Peter found a rock as big as his hand could hold. Then, bracing the coconut between his knees, he hammered the knife blade into the tough shell.

"There!" he cried, finally breaking through. He handed the first coconut to Oliver, who greedily drained it dry in big gulps.

Then Peter drilled into the second green nut and drank from it. "This is delicious!" he cried. "And so sweet. I can hardly believe such nectar lives inside this strange, furry fruit!"

Peter then used Oliver's cutlass to open a third nut. He and Oliver shared the white, flaky meat.

"Now we have two nice bowls to eat our insects from!" Oliver joked when they were done.

"No bugs for me," Peter smiled. "But I've been thinking. Perhaps I can make a spear using your knife blade. Then I can wade out into the water and spear some fish."

"You'll probably not find fish this close to shore," Oliver said.

"Maybe crabs then," Peter said. "When the tide goes out, I'll look for them."

"I hope you're right, laddie," Oliver replied.

At midday, the two friends rested in the shade of the palm tree.

"What do you think will become of us?" Peter asked Oliver.

"We will perish within the year if we are not found," the young pirate replied. "Some storm will take us into the sea, and we will drown. Some of these gales wash right over little islands like this one. The ocean just swallows them up for a while. Or maybe we'll run out of coconuts. We can't compete with the monkeys for them. There are too many of them and not enough of us."

"Do no ships at all come this way?" Peter asked.

"The *Infamy*'s the only ship that would come close to the island," Oliver said bitterly. "The crew members are the only ones who know we're here. And I doubt that any of them would want to rescue us."

"Have you ever marooned a man?" Peter asked quietly.

Oliver hesitated. Then he said, "Not on my own, but I was part of a crew that once did. The captain of our vessel found one of the men keeping treasure we had taken for himself. We took the poor devil to an island and left him there. I can still hear his cries, but at the time I didn't care . . . "

"Did you ever find out what happened to the man?" Peter asked.

"Sometime later we returned to the island and found a skeleton on the beach. We figured it was probably his remains," Oliver said.

Peter shuddered. "What a vicious thing to do. I cannot imagine any man coarse of soul enough to be a buccaneer."

Riley Oliver said nothing, but Peter thought he noticed a look of regret in his eyes.

When the midday heat passed, Peter waded into the sea hoping to spot some fish. Then he'd attempt to make a spear from Oliver's knife. But there were no fish to be found. There were no signs of crabs either.

Disappointed, he returned to the higher ground where Oliver waited.

"What if we build a small boat?" Peter wondered aloud.

"Out of bits and pieces of palm fronds and driftwood?" Oliver asked skeptically.

Peter nodded in agreement. "You're right," he admitted. "The only real source of wood here is the palm trees. And we have no way to cut one down, let alone fashion it into a boat." He sighed then and said, "Are you as hungry as I am?"

The pirate nodded.

"I'll crack open another of the coconuts then," Peter said. "At least we have something to keep us going for awhile."

After they had eaten, Peter checked Oliver's wound again. He was pleased to see that it was mending nicely.

"I have to thank you again, Peter," Oliver said. "Without your knowledge of healing, I would probably be dead."

Peter smiled ruefully. "Saving your life was for naught if we never get off this island," he pointed out.

"Ah, well, I've made myself a good friend in the meantime," Oliver said. "You know, I don't believe I've ever had a friend, Peter. Never had the kind of childhood that allowed for friends. And I certainly never trusted any of my shipmates. You're my first friend, young Peter McCall."

"Let's hope I'm not your last," Peter replied.

They slept then and awoke to a red dawn.

"Red sky in the morning, sailor's warning," Oliver said as they ate the last of the coconuts. "The only question is, how bad will it be?"

"We'd better find the highest spot on the island, just in case," Peter said. "And if the storm hits, we'll need to hang on to something. Lash ourselves to tree trunks, if necessary. We can use our shirts again, maybe even our trousers."

Oliver smiled. "You have a wonderful will to live, boy. Where does it come from?" he asked.

"From my ambitions, I suppose," Peter replied. "I plan to do something special with my life. I intend to be a doctor. I want to help people—not just those who can afford to pay, but the indigent as well. There are so many exciting developments taking place in medicine today—new remedies, treatments. I want to be a part of it. I can't do that if I'm stuck here on this island. I need to keep myself alive on the chance that we may leave here someday."

"I admire you, laddie," Oliver said.

"What will you do if we are rescued?" Peter asked.

"I've been giving that some thought," Oliver answered. "The way I look at it, if we get off this island, it'll be like a second chance for me. You don't get many second chances in life, Peter. So I've decided I'd better take advantage of it. No more pirating for me, I promise you. I'll be going straight from now on."

"I'm glad to hear that," Peter said. "Where do you think you will live?"

"I'll probably go to Charles Town to be near Caroline. Since she's the only family I have," Oliver replied. "Perhaps I can take up a trade there—become a wheelwright or even a tinsmith like my father."

"That's wonderful," Peter said. "Those are honorable professions. And Caroline will be happy to have you nearby again, I'm sure."

The thought of Caroline made Peter realize he wanted to get off the island more than ever. He wanted a chance to get to know her better. Before he'd met her, he hadn't realized that women could be so independent. His mother and sisters relied upon the men in their lives to make decisions of any importance for them. But Caroline was different. She loved Oliver, but she was not about to let him tell her what to do. Peter thought Caroline was the type of woman he'd want to marry someday—maybe *the* woman he wanted to marry.

Carrying the few supplies they had in Peter's herb sack, they climbed to the highest point on the island. From there they could see the horizon in all directions. If a storm came, they would spot it long before it hit.

By midday, thin clouds began building to the west, but the sea remained perfectly calm. It was hard for Peter to believe that such still waters might soon become dangerous. The air grew heavy and hot, and the sky took on a reddish cast.

Peter noticed how quiet the island was. The only sound was the rhythmic surge of the waves as they lazily lapped the shore. He glanced into the treetops. The monkeys, whose chatter had been almost constant, were gone. Peter wondered where they might have escaped to on such a small island. He hoped they were safe.

At dusk, a line of black clouds joined the thin clouds, and a warm breeze gusted now and then, rippling the calm sea. The waves gained strength, and the palm trees rustled above them.

Still Peter felt no great danger. It seemed to be a storm and nothing more. "Perhaps it will even blow over us," he suggested to Oliver.

But Oliver shook his head. "Just the opposite," he replied. "The way I read those clouds, it's headed right for us. And it's a bad one—maybe even a hurricane. Better lash yourself down now."

Peter did as he was told. First he lashed

the herb sack to a tree. Then he used the sling he had made the day before to bind himself to a tree. He pulled the sling more tightly, though, so that his body was close against the tree trunk. Oliver used his trousers to tie himself to a tree nearby.

No sooner had they gotten themselves secured than the wind turned cool. And with it came great spattering drops of rain. Peter looked up and saw massive dark clouds roiling above the island. The wind began whipping the tops of the palm trees into a frenzy. It drove crashing waves onto the shore.

Peter watched as the water crept farther and farther up the beach. After a quarter of an hour, he looked at where their old campsite had been. It was completely under water!

Bullets of rain pelted them from above. Peter could hardly believe the stinging pain on his back and head. It felt as if someone were shooting hard, little peas at him at close range.

Suddenly a great wall of waves hit the beach. Water flooded the island, not 20 yards from where they stood.

"Hold on to the tree!" Oliver yelled. "The next one might reach us!"

Peter ducked his head and grasped the tree trunk with all the strength in his arms and legs. The surf roared mightily again. Suddenly he felt the sand beneath his feet disappear. He clung desperately to the palm. But the next wave hit him with such force that it pulled the sling apart. A few seconds later, Peter found himself being carried out to sea. The heaving, foaming ocean stretched out endlessly before him. He clawed out for something to hang on to, but there was nothing.

I'm drowning, Peter thought. After all this, I am going to drown in the sea!

10 The wave crested and rolled, and Peter went under, gulping water. He tried desperately to head back to the island, but where was it? he wondered. Everything seemed to belong to the sea. The dark storm had swallowed up the palm trees, and Peter could see nothing. He had been tossed and turned so many times that he had lost his sense of direction.

Suddenly a hand reached out from the dark sea, and powerful fingers grasped Peter's arm.

"This way!" Oliver shouted over the roar of the water.

Peter swam with all his might. He was to the point of exhaustion when he realized that he did not have to struggle quite so much against the surf. As fast as the storm had come up, it was dying down.

Peter felt sand beneath his feet, and he stumbled ashore, dropping to his knees on the beach. After a minute, he looked around. Oliver was just coming out of the water, only a few yards away.

Peter coughed violently and spit out

mouthfuls of saltwater. "Are you all right?" he finally gasped. He could see that Oliver's wound had been torn open. A stream of blood was running down his side.

"Yes," Oliver panted, pressing his hand against his wound. "I think that was the worst of it. Are you all right, laddie?"

"Yes," Peter said, coughing some more. "Thanks for helping me. I would have been swept out to sea if not for you."

"I owed you that, Peter—and far, far more," Oliver said.

The next waves were less powerful. Each successive wave was weaker until at last the sea calmed. As if on signal, a bright moon moved out from the cloud bank.

The two friends moved up the beach a ways and collapsed onto the sand. "I wish I could dress that wound," Peter said. "But my herb sack was surely taken by the storm."

"I'll be all right, laddie," Oliver assured him. "The wound was healing nicely, and I doubt that a little sea water is going to bother it much."

Peter ached in every bone of his body. He had never been so tired and sore and was soon sound asleep.

At dawn the next morning, Oliver shook Peter awake. "Peter, get up!" he said. "I see something in the distance, but I'm afraid to believe my own eyes!"

Peter sat up and rubbed his eyes. He felt as if he'd only slept an hour. "What is it?" he asked groggily.

Oliver pointed out to sea and said, "Is that an illusion, a trick of my maddened brain, or is there a ship on the horizon?"

Peter jumped to his feet, his exhaustion leaving him instantly. "It *is* a ship!" he cried. "Maybe the storm blew her off course!"

"But how will we attract her attention?" Oliver asked. "She'll never see us!"

Peter ran down to the water's edge, waving his arms wildly. But he knew Oliver was right. They couldn't possibly be seen from so great a distance.

He looked desperately around him. What wood that had washed up on the beach was wet. There was no time to build a fire anyway. Unless the ship were moving toward them, it would be out of sight in a matter of minutes. How could they make themselves be seen?

He groaned and said, "They'll never see us. They're probably eager to get back on course and are not even looking this way."

"Don't lose your spirit *now*, laddie," Oliver urged him. "First let's figure out which way she's headed." He squinted his eyes. "Can you make out the flags she wears?"

"No, she's too far away," Peter said.

"Wait!" Oliver gasped. "She's coming closer! Isn't she coming closer, laddie? Are my eyes deceiving me? Look sharp now!"

Peter stared at the spot in the distance. It *did* appear to be getting bigger.

"You're right!" he cried. "The ship is coming this way! The wind must be pushing her, for why else would she come to this island?"

"It looks to me that the ship moves in this direction purposefully," Oliver said. "And now I see the flags. She sails under the Union Jack. She's British!"

"We're going to be rescued!" Peter shouted joyfully.

"Or arrested and hanged as pirates," Oliver said. "I'll tell them you were the prisoner of pirates so that they will not hang you, Peter. But I expect I'll soon be swinging from a hangman's noose."

"No," Peter said. "I'm the only one who could accuse you, Oliver, and I never will. You hauled me the sea and saved my life. We'll stick together—no matter what!"

"But what you've gone through because of me—" Oliver began.

"That's over now," Peter said. "Over and forgotten."

"Is there no end to your generosity, boy?" Oliver asked in wonder.

"Our story shall be that we were on a merchant ship headed to the West Indies when a storm took her down. We were washed ashore here," Peter said. "Agreed?"

Oliver clapped Peter on the back. "Agreed!" he said.

Half an hour later, the *Duchess* dropped anchor off the coast of the island. A small boat was lowered over the side. It was manned by two British seamen, who rowed toward the small island.

"Hello, mates," one of the seamen hailed.

"Hello!" Peter cried, wading out to meet them. "What a blessed sight you are! How did you find us?"

"We put ashore in Barbados a few days ago," the first seaman explained. "We came across an old sailor with a wild tale to tell. He said he'd seen castaways on this island. His captain would not stop to check, he said, for they had been blown off course and were in a great hurry to deliver their goods. We doubted him, for he was a rummy to be sure. Looked more like a buccaneer than a sailor. But our captain decided to check out the tale. He himself had been cast away once. He knew the predicament you'd be in if indeed you were here. Looks like the old man was speaking the truth."

Peter and Oliver looked at each other, puzzled. No ship had passed by the island since they had been marooned. They were sure of that.

"Did the sailor tell his name?" Oliver asked.

"No, but another called him Eli," the sailor replied.

Eli Cooper! Peter thought. Old Eli must have watched the duel and the marooning from the deck of the *Infamy*. The first chance he got, he sent help.

Peter shook his head and smiled. All because of a small act of kindness, he thought. An herb to ease a stomachache.

"You chaps ready to get off this island?" the other seaman asked.

"Are we ever!" Peter exclaimed.

He and Oliver climbed into the boat. The two sailors turned the little craft around and headed toward the *Duchess*. On the way, Peter glanced back at the little island. He could see no sign that they had been there. All evidence of the violent duel between Oliver and Seth Hanes had been washed away. And there were no signs of the camp he and Oliver had set up under the trees.

They were leaving the island as they had found it—an unspoiled paradise. He glanced up at the treetops and saw movement. The monkeys! They had made it through the storm and were back at work gathering coconuts.

Peter waved farewell to them and

turned back toward the *Duchess*. He was finally going home!

* * *

Peter and Riley Oliver were taken to Charles Town, South Carolina, (which later became Charleston). Oliver convinced Peter to stay with him and Caroline for a few days before returning to Boston. The few days became a month, and during that time, Peter and Caroline fell in love. When Peter finally left, Caroline promised that she would wait for his return.

A few months later, Peter went to Cambridge to study medicine. He returned to the colonies a doctor. A year later, he and Caroline were married and settled in Boston.

Riley Oliver declined his new brother-in-law's invitation to join them in Massachusetts. He preferred instead to work at building up the tinsmith business he had started. Oliver became very successful and eventually built the house he'd always wanted—with honest money.

Peter lived up to his ambition as well. Besides becoming a well-respected doctor, he and Caroline started an orphanage for the poor children of Boston. Their aim was to help children like Riley Oliver who would have otherwise grown up on the streets alone.

Piracy was eventually eliminated, but not before the crew of the *Infamy* was captured and brought before an Admiralty Court. All the men, including Eli Cooper, were hanged.

Novels by Anne Schraff

PASSAGES
An Alien Spring
Bridge to the Moon (Sequel to *Maitland's Kid*)
The Darkest Secret
Don't Blame the Children
The Ghost Boy
The Haunting of Hawthorne
Maitland's Kid
Please Don't Ask Me to Love You
The Power of the Rose (Sequel to *The
    Haunting of Hawthorne*)
The Shadow Man
The Shining Mark (Sequel to *When a Hero Dies*)
A Song to Sing
Sparrow's Treasure
Summer of Shame (Sequel to *An Alien Spring*)
To Slay the Dragon (Sequel to *Don't Blame
    the Children*)
The Vandal
When a Hero Dies

PASSAGES 2000
The Boy from Planet Nowhere
Gingerbread Heart
The Hyena Laughs at Night
Just Another Name for Lonely (Sequel to
    Please Don't Ask Me to Love You)
Memories Are Forever

PASSAGES to History
And We Will Be No More
The Bloody Wake of the *Infamy*
Dear Mr. Kilmer
Dream Mountain
Hear That Whistle Blow
Strawberry Autumn
Winter at Wolf Crossing
The Witches of Northboro